Blooming
Through Thorns

Blooming Through Thorns
Cherie Hans

Copyright © 2025 Cherie Hans

All rights reserved. No part of this publication may be reproduced, distributed, or transmitted in any form or by any means, including photocopying, recording, or other electronic or mechanical methods, without the prior written permission from the author, except in the case of brief quotations embodied in critical reviews and certain other noncommercial uses permitted by copyright law.

This book is a work of fiction. Names, characters, businesses, organizations, places, and events other than those clearly in the public domain are either the product of the author's imagination or used fictitiously. Any resemblance to actual persons (living or dead), events, or locales is purely coincidental.

ISBN: 979-8-9927143-3-3

Editor: Ita de Groot
Cover Design: Lesia @GermanCreative
Formatting: Brady Moller

Blooming Through Thorns

CHERIE HANS

I dedicate this book to my brother, Gary, who did not live to see this published.

PART 1

CHAPTER ONE

THE DAY SHE LEFT

Emma escaped on a scorching, dank day. She gathered her cats, computer, and clothing, her hands trembling as she stuffed items into bags. With each drawer she emptied, she reclaimed her dignity.

The night before, she had asked Chad if they could go for counseling to attempt to repair their shattered marriage. His retort had been swift and cruel. "All therapists are quacks, and two of you bitches aren't going to tell me what to do!"

She thanked him silently for being consistent and making her decision easier.

Emma had already called her friend, Laura, the day before. She knew that Chad would never go to therapy, and she knew she would be leaving. Laura had offered to help Emma leave him when she was ready. Emma trusted Laura—they had met in seventh grade and were thick as thieves.

The day Emma left, their apartment felt peaceful in Chad's absence. Sunlight peeked through the edges of the pristine white blinds—blinds he never allowed her to open, convinced that sunlight would create dust. Even the most minor decisions weren't hers to make.

The air felt different that day, lighter somehow, despite the summer humidity that usually made their apartment feel like a pressure cooker. Even the worn floorboards beneath her feet seemed to creak in encouragement as she moved from room to room, gathering the fragments of her life into those telling black garbage bags.

For a moment, Emma could breathe, though her heart raced with every sound that might signal his return.

A FEW WEEKS EARLIER, CHAD HAD GONE BALLISTIC BECAUSE Emma had a few inches cut off her long hair without his permission. When he went into his rages, she usually remained silent, as even exhaling too loudly would make things worse. Feeling defiant this time, Emma had shouted, "Just because you're losing your hair doesn't mean you can live vicariously through mine!"

She paid for that quip. A hand wrapped around her throat, and the other formed a fist in her face. She told Chad that if he touched her, she would go to the police before the hospital. She believed that his threats were real.

Emma's heart hammered against her ribs as the pressure on her throat tightened. Black dots swarmed at the edges of her vision. The room seemed to shrink around her, and she could feel her pulse pounding in her ears as terror flooded her system. She didn't dare move. Emma did not know why, but he finally let go. Her legs nearly buckled beneath her as she gasped for air, her hand instinctively moving to her throat.

Chad reminded her how lucky she was that he didn't drink or cheat. "You're so lucky to have me," he said, his voice eerily calm compared to moments before.

Emma was so lucky. That's what she was supposed to believe. She didn't go to the police, and since he didn't hit her, she didn't have to go to the hospital. There were no physical marks, only the invisible scars of fear etched deeper into her psyche. For Emma, this physical threat of violence was the last straw. She had never been hit before, and this was not going to be the first time.

Despite this violent and frightening episode, Emma did not leave the next day. She was petrified, but her cats, Oscar and Ziggy, were her priority. Every time she looked at their trusting eyes, she felt a knot in her stomach. Chad constantly said he would toss them outside. "One day, you'll come home, and they'll be gone," he'd threaten casually, as if discussing the weather. They had been indoor cats for their whole lives. They would not survive outside for one moment. The thought of them lost, scared, and alone paralyzed her with guilt and dread.

Emma started thinking more seriously about leaving him, but she felt paralyzed and trapped. She'd lie awake at night, mapping escape routes in her mind, only to have them dissolve by morning. Every day, Chad told her what a loser she would be if she left. "You're nothing without me," he'd remind her over breakfast, lunch, and dinner—a poisonous mantra served with every meal. Being in Connecticut, away from everybody she knew, made everything seem insurmountable. The isolation surrounded her like a fog, making even the most straightforward decisions feel impossible.

THE NIGHT BEFORE SHE LEFT, SHE LAY AWAKE, PRETENDING EVerything was copacetic to protect Oscar and Ziggy for one final night. The boys were Emma's cats before she and Chad had wed, and he constantly threatened to hurt them to control her. She had to get them out safely.

The logistics were complex. Laura was allergic to cats, and Emma's new apartment wouldn't be ready for two weeks. Emma's dear friends, Kim and John, who loved cats and lived in Queens, had agreed to babysit Oscar and Ziggy until her new space was ready.

In an era before smartphones and texting, planning the escape felt surreal. Chad would walk in while she was emailing—phone calls were too risky—and she'd have to hit "send" mid-sentence, piecing together her plan through countless fragmented messages.

"How will we get all my clothes out of the house?" Emma had asked Laura that morning.

Her friend's sardonic smile spoke volumes. "In big, black garbage bags. That should kill him in front of the neighbors!"

So, Emma packed her things in black garbage bags to expedite leaving her ex. As she stuffed her clothes and personal items into the crinkly plastic, a small, bitter smile crossed her lips. She realized why her friend had suggested this tactic—the black garbage bags would embarrass him in front of the neighbors. In Chad's manicured Connecticut neighborhood, appearances weren't just important; they were everything. Chad was a Connecticut man through and through, his family's roots stretching back generations in New England soil. He wore his heritage like armor, name-dropping prep schools and referring to summer homes with practiced casualness. The thought of neighbors seeing garbage bags being carried from his pristine colonial would mortify him more than the actual act of her leaving. His carefully cultivated image—the successful businessman with the perfect life—couldn't withstand such a pedestrian display. The more chaotic and "low-class" her exit appeared, the less likely he'd be to make a scene. His pride wouldn't allow it.

She knew his weakness well: Chad would rather die than have the Richardsons across the street or the Hiltons down the block witness anything that suggested disorder in his perfect life. His machismo required control, refinement, and old-money discretion—not black plastic bags and messy departures. It was the one card Emma had left to play, and she was going to use it.

There was a glimmer of triumph in stuffing her carefully maintained wardrobe, hangers and all, into those industrial trash bags.

Chad pretended to go to a doctor's appointment on the morning of her departure—he suspected something was amiss.

The day Emma was preparing to meet Laura to find an apartment, he returned earlier than expected, entering their bedroom. He tried to close the door to talk, but Emma ignored him and kept stuffing her clothes into black garbage bags. The hinges creaked as Chad pushed the door halfway shut, his voice dropping into that honeyed tone she'd recognized as manipulation.

"Emma, please. Can't we sit down and discuss this like adults?" He leaned against the doorframe, his body language casual but his eyes calculating. She could feel his gaze on her back as she methodically continued packing. She shoved another shirt into the bag, refusing to look up at him. When she didn't respond, he stepped further into the room, his hand still on the doorknob. "Come on, you're overreacting. Let me make you some tea, and we can talk about this." The same hands that had been around her throat were now being offered in supposed peace.

Emma's fingers trembled slightly, but she didn't pause in her packing. She knew this script too well—the apologies that weren't apologies, the promises that dissolved like sugar in rain.

Emma found her voice. "If you close it, Laura will call the police."

Believe it or not, finding an apartment that accepts two cats was not easy. And Emma did not know how to get around Connecticut. She'd been living there for a year, but Chad drove circuitously to confuse her. She had to memorize routes since there were no GPS devices in those days, and she always got lost inside a shoebox. And because Chad intentionally drove indirect routes, she only knew how to go to three places: her gym, the high school where she worked, and home to I-95.

Their marital possessions remained behind, especially her now worthless wedding dress—a heap of white fluff on the floor.

Emma was leaving a voicemail on her Uncle Denny and Aunt Carol's phone when Chad came in screaming at her and cursing—telling her to hang up. His face was contorted with rage as he burst through the doorway, the sudden intrusion making her flinch. The phone trembled in her hand as his shouting filled the room.

"Hang up that fucking phone right now!" Chad's voice thundered as he lunged toward her, spittle flying from his mouth.

Emma instinctively backed against the wall, the phone still clutched to her ear, her aunt's voicemail still recording. As Chad's tirade continued, the calm message she'd been leaving about possibly visiting soon shattered into fragments.

Her throat closed up, words dying before they could form. What could she possibly say now? "Oh, Aunt Carol, don't mind the screaming man threatening me in the background?" She knew she couldn't explain his disgusting behavior to her family. They had only seen the charming, polished version of Chad at holiday gatherings and family events. They'd never believe this was the same man who'd proudly discussed sailing at Martha's Vineyard and quoted Thoreau over Thanksgiving dinner.

Emma's thumb hovered over the "End Call" button. The humiliation of having her aunt hear this burned hot on her face, but a small, desperate part of her almost wanted to keep the line open—to have someone, anyone, witness what her life had become. Shame won out. She ended the call abruptly, her eyes fixed on Chad's contorted face.

In that moment, looking at the stranger before her, she knew she had to leave. Not tomorrow, not next week—today. The realization settled into her bones with a cold certainty. No more excuses, no more delays. This would not be her life.

Emma left the vacation package they had planned on the kitchen table and was relieved she wasn't going. Spending a week trapped with Chad on a ship felt more like boarding the *Titanic* than a luxury cruise.

She didn't have to say she was no longer afraid of him; it was apparent. His weapon had been keeping their secret, keeping his abuse quiet—not his threats. Once she realized this, she found the courage to leave.

CHAPTER TWO

HOW THEY MET

Emma's friends were all getting married and starting to have kids. In the 1990s, many were still getting married in their twenties, hosting bridal showers in restaurants' party rooms and browsing through thick wedding magazines at Barnes & Noble. Emma was twenty-nine; societal pressure squeezed her tightly back then, showing up in subtle ways. For example, the knowing looks at weddings when she sat at the singles table, the gentle inquiries about whether she was "seeing anyone special."

Emma's mom gifted her a home computer. On her teaching salary, she could not have afforded it and was grateful. They were monster-sized desktops then and expensive—a Dell that hummed and took up half her desk. With it, she registered with an online dating site, spending hours crafting a profile that wouldn't make her sound desperate or too eager.

It wasn't that she lacked judgment—she'd deleted dozens of messages before his appeared in her inbox. There were the overly aggressive men with their thinly veiled sexual propositions disguised as compliments. The ones who couldn't string together a coherent sentence, typing "ur beautiful" with no further substance. The married men "just looking for friends" whose profiles mysteriously lacked photos. Then there were the endless silent rejections—messages she'd crafted carefully to interesting prospects that vanished into the digital void without response.

By the time Chad's message arrived, Emma had been on the dating site for six months. Six months of awkward coffee dates with men who looked nothing like their grainy, low-resolution photos. Six months of conversations that stalled after fifteen minutes. One particularly memorable disaster involved a man who spent an entire dinner detailing his collection of Star Trek memorabilia while never once asking her a question about herself.

The bar had been set so low that she ignored the small warning signs: his slightly condescending tone when discussing her job, his insistence on planning their first date entirely on his terms. Emma, exhausted by the parade of losers and ghosters, mistook his controlling nature for confidence. By the time she recognized what it truly was, she was already entangled in his web, far from home, with his ring on her finger.

As a teacher who spent her days correcting her English language learners' fourth-grade writing, she wasn't thrilled to meet a man online who didn't capitalize his letters or use punctuation. Her students wrote better. His messages read like hasty text messages before texting was even a thing.

She told herself to stop being so picky, or she would always be alone—another sore point that kept her awake at night, staring at her bedroom ceiling.

Chad did not live in New York but in Connecticut—not too far, but another state she knew very little about. Thinking it would not go anywhere, she reluctantly answered his message, her fingers hovering over the keyboard before finally hitting "Send."

Emma was relieved to see him in person on the evening of their first date at a chain restaurant just off the I-95. Chad stood at an impressive six feet three, his blond hair neatly styled, the kind of effortless perfection that came from years of knowing exactly how to present himself. His gray eyes were sharp and unreadable, a remarkable contrast to the warmth of his sun-kissed skin. He wore ironed jeans, crisp and immaculate despite their casual nature, paired with a pink Tommy Hilfiger polo that hinted at old money and summers spent on the Connecticut coast. On his feet, he sported Sperry's, those classic boat shoes worn without socks—a staple of preppy confidence. There was an ease about him that came from privilege, but whether it made him charming or insufferable depended entirely on the observer.

At five feet three, Emma moved with the fluid confidence of someone who had spent years in front of a classroom. Her long, straight, strawberry blonde hair caught the light when she walked, sometimes appearing more golden, other times reflecting hints of copper. She typically wore it loose but pulled it back in a simple ponytail while teaching.

Her gray eyes, bright and alert, had a way of focusing intently on whoever she was speaking with, making her students feel genuinely heard.

Though she kept her nails short and practical but always polished professionally, there was an undeniable feminine grace about her that had nothing to do with artifice. She didn't bother with more than eye makeup; she abhorred facial makeup that always looked caked on. She let her natural coloring and fitness speak for themselves.

Emma was a more down-to-earth casual dresser compared to Chad. Also, she came from divorced parents (Chad would rub that in as often as possible) in a middle-class neighborhood. They were a comfortable, educated family, unlike Chad's. She thought for sure this date would be a one-and-done. That he would want a woman who was like himself.

They both worked out often, so he was fit too, filling out his polo shirt in a way that made other women in the restaurant glance over. That was where the bonuses ended, though she wouldn't admit it to herself then. Emma never enjoyed dating a man who dressed better than her. She would later discover that he needed more time to prep than she did—a sore spot in their time together.

Emma had chosen navy blue sparkly nail polish because it was her favorite and caught the light when she moved her hands. Chad preferred more traditional, safe colors, and he told her so that first night together—his eyes fixed on her fingers with disapproval as she reached for her water glass. It should have been a red flag, but as she was turning thirty soon, she persevered, quietly tucking her hands under the table.

They fell into a dating routine: Friday night movies, Sunday brunches at places Chad chose, nightly phone calls. But Emma said no the night Chad asked if he could sleep over because it was a long interstate ride home. She felt she would do something right in this relationship and hold on to her principles. They had only been dating for a few weeks. He was incensed, his face turning a shade of red she'd never seen before. It was frightening the way his knuckles whitened around his car keys.

The next day, Chad told Emma that as he drove home, navigating the dark highway, he had decided to make their relationship official because he admired her strong principles. The way he could flip from fury to admiration made her stomach twist, but she smiled anyway.

Chapter Three

VALENTINE'S DAY

Isn't Valentine's Day the most romantic day for couples? Emma and Chad had only been dating for a few months—still in the honeymoon period—so it should have been the perfect day for two twenty-somethings. But we're talking about Chad, so it went downhill fast and was a day Emma would dread every year from then on.

After dedicating a decade to teaching in New York City public schools, Emma received an unexpected job offer on Long Island in the suburbs. The opportunity arose when she met the principal of a Long Island school district. The principal, learning of Emma's background, asked if she would consider becoming their Spanish teacher.

Until then, Emma had worked as a bilingual Spanish teacher in Queens, teaching elementary-aged English language learners English while instructing them in Spanish in core subjects—math, reading, writing, and science. Her path hadn't been easy; she had substituted for nearly two years before getting a long-term position. Emma accepted the position teaching Spanish to seventh and eighth graders at two Long Island middle schools. Her new schedule split up her teaching day: mornings at one middle school and afternoons at the other.

As Valentine's Day approached, Chad, unfamiliar with Long Island, asked Emma for a local florist's business card near her schools, planning to send her flowers. In hindsight, his gesture seemed more about public display than Emma's happiness.

That Valentine's Day evening, Chad drove to Emma's home in Queens for dinner, arriving visibly agitated that she hadn't effusively thanked him. Confused, Emma learned he had sent flowers to her. Though she hadn't received any, she was touched by the thought.

What should have been a romantic evening devolved into a bitter argument. Chad blamed Emma, claiming the florist's card she'd provided was from an untrustworthy business that had taken his money without delivering. His anger escalated despite Emma's assurances about the florist's reputation and offer to investigate the mishap.

While many twenty-nine-year-olds might have been upset about not receiving anything for Valentine's Day, Emma's maturity showed in her response. She focused on Chad's intention rather than the outcome, promising to visit the shop the next day to sort things out.

Chad's reaction was disproportionate. His rage targeted Emma directly, ruining their evening as she struggled to maintain composure across the dinner table.

The following day, Emma discovered her delivery had been mishandled due to her split schedule between two schools. The manager fully refunded Chad's payment and insisted Emma accept a dozen beautiful red roses despite her initial reluctance.

Even with the situation resolved and no actual harm done, Chad's anger persisted. He spent the following week berating Emma by phone—their living arrangements still separate—holding her responsible for circumstances beyond her control. It became a familiar pattern: anything that displeased Chad somehow became Emma's fault, leaving her confused but increasingly resigned to the dynamic.

CHAPTER

Four

THE PROPOSAL

Their relationship continued, and a year later, Chad proposed at the Empire State Building. He got down on one knee on the observation deck, and everyone stopped to watch. Thankfully, there were no smartphones back then. Emma was mortified and begged him to stand up, feeling the weight of strangers' eyes on her back. Was this a normal reaction? Of course she said yes, but reluctantly, her voice barely a whisper.

Chad had been acting strangely all that day and evening, checking his pants pocket every few minutes and barely touching his lunch. Now she knew why. Also, he hated Manhattan and complained constantly about the crowds and the noise (her fault), so she was surprised he had insisted on sightseeing that afternoon.

Emma's new two-carat engagement ring sparkled and was spectacular, catching every bit of light like a disco ball on her finger. Chad loved disco music, but Emma was a rock 'n' roll kind of girl. He always wanted to go dancing, and she dreaded it. The ring was not to Emma's taste since she was a sensible New York City gal who did not want an expensive ring that would call attention to her. The ring served two purposes: to lock her in and to impress everyone else with what a generous guy Chad was.

It was her first official proposal with an actual ring, though, so Emma thought Chad was the only man who would ever want her. She felt like she was damaged goods, though she couldn't point to when she started feeling that way. She didn't know why, but she had this overwhelming feeling of doom, like dark clouds gathering on the horizon.

Chad's family was thrilled to hear the news; his mother was already discussing venues and flower arrangements. Emma's side, not so much—their congratulations came with worried eyes and careful questions about whether she was sure. Once they were engaged, the wedding wheels of motion started spinning, picking up speed like a runaway train, and she didn't know how to stop them or if she even should.

Chapter Five

THE ENGAGEMENT PERIOD

Their time together was limited to one night during the week and weekends, creating a pressure-cooker environment where every moment in this interstate relationship had to be perfect. But Emma would learn that perfection was defined solely by Chad's standards.

Arguments erupted over everything—the restaurants they chose, the shows they watched, even the way Emma laughed at a joke. The geographic distance between them served as both a blessing and a curse. While it provided Emma with breathing room, it also made it harder for her to see the pattern forming. Like looking at a mosaic from too close, she could see each piece but struggled to recognize the disturbing picture they created together.

During their brief time together, Chad's jealousy manifested in increasingly controlling behaviors. At Emma's local gym, where she had been a member for years, a familiar trainer approached to correct her form during a dead lift. Chad's reaction was immediate and disproportionate. His face flushed red as he stepped between them, loudly questioning the trainer's professionalism and Emma's judgment. The scene he created left Emma mortified, her cheeks burning with embarrassment in front of the morning regulars she'd known for years. After that, Emma decided they wouldn't work out together on weekends to avoid another conflict, ending her cherished routine. The gym had been her sanctuary; now it had become another battleground where she had to choose between peace and personal freedom. After this experience, Emma stopped going to the gym with Chad. He'd only gone there a couple of times with her before he ruined it. Now she could only go on weekdays when he wasn't around.

Chad began pushing for an earlier wedding date as winter melted into spring. His seemingly romantic urgency masked a deeper motivation that Emma wouldn't recognize until much later—the need to secure his control before she could fully grasp what was happening. Each time she suggested they take more time to plan, he would remind her how much he loved her and couldn't bear to wait, his words sweet but laced with an underlying desperation that should have been a warning.

Obviously, Emma had seen signs that Chad was abusive before they got married. The evidence was there in a hundred small moments—the way he criticized her outfits, how he'd check her phone when he thought she wasn't looking, his subtle digs about her friends being "bad influences." But she didn't know then what it was or what it was called. The individual incidents seemed minor to her, easily dismissed as quirks or him having bad days. It wasn't until years later that she would recognize them as textbook red flags—the early warning signs she kept on ignoring, thinking they would get better in time. But Chad's control and anger only grew and got worse.

She was twenty-nine going on thirty, and all her friends were married. Emma's biological clock wasn't just ticking—it was practically screaming. Every family gathering brought the inevitable questions: "Meeting anyone special?" "Still single?" Each one landed like a tiny accusation.

With her twenties slipping away, the prospect of being alone terrified her more than Chad's controlling behavior. She felt societal pressure and ignored the signs, filing away each uncomfortable moment under "things we'll work on after the wedding."

She also lacked self-esteem, which she wouldn't uncover during therapy until after she left him. Years of putting herself last had hollowed her out, leaving her unable to recognize her own worth. She'd come to believe Chad's narrative—that she was lucky to have him, that she was difficult to love, that his criticism was just "helping her improve."

It wasn't until she sat across from her therapist, months after leaving, that she finally named the void inside her. "You've never learned to value yourself," the therapist had said gently. Emma had cried then, not from sadness but recognition—the pieces of the puzzle finally shifting into place.

The question of where they would live after the marriage loomed large in Emma's mind. Connecticut represented more than just geographic distance—it meant leaving behind the life she'd carefully built for herself. After years of dedicated work, she finally achieved tenure at her school, a professional milestone that brought security and pride. Her family lived close enough for impromptu visits, and her friends were a source of comfort. The thought of transplanting herself to Connecticut filled her with a dread she tried to ignore.

Even her long-held dietary choices became subject to Chad's control. When they first met, he had seemed fascinated by her veganism, asking seemingly thoughtful questions about her reasons. But as his true nature emerged, that fascination turned to criticism. "I can't be with someone who doesn't eat meat," he declared one evening over dinner, his tone casual but his eyes hard. "It's just not normal."

The first time Emma forced herself to eat chicken, she nearly gagged. For their three years together, Emma reluctantly ate meat again. Every bit of fat, blood, or vein irked her, but she needed to conform, so she did, against all her beliefs and feelings. Chad beamed with approval, and she found herself swallowing the meat and her values, telling herself this compromise was part of loving someone.

Her appearance became another battlefield. Emma's long hair, which she'd always worn up in hot and humid weather, became a point of contention.

"I love seeing your hair down," Chad would say, reaching over to unclip her hair. "I like it better this way."

The compliment carried an implicit threat—her beauty was conditional on his preferences. Even as summer temperatures soared, she learned to keep her hair down, her neck damp with sweat, but her boyfriend was satisfied.

Day by day, piece by piece, Emma felt herself dissolving into a version of herself designed to please Chad. Like water gradually wearing away stone, his constant criticism and control eroded her sense of self. The woman who had once confidently navigated her own life now second-guessed everything, looking to Chad for approval before making even the most minor decision. Her transformation into his ideal partner was nearly complete, but the cost was the loss of everything that had made her uniquely Emma.

Chapter Six

THE WEDDING PLANNING

Let's start with the dress. Emma's mother reluctantly accompanied her to what felt like every bridal shop in New York. After endless appointments and growing frustration, they finally found a long gown in off-white with blue roses embroidered throughout the fabric. The moment Emma stepped out of the dressing room, her mother's eyes softened, and for a brief moment, both women allowed themselves to feel the joy this occasion should have brought.

That joy shattered the moment Emma mentioned the dress to Chad. He went ballistic, his voice rising with each word. "Off-white? What kind of bride doesn't wear pure white? And blue flowers? It is our wedding; it isn't a barbeque!"

His reaction only escalated when she admitted she hadn't planned on wearing a veil.

"Every bride wears a veil," he insisted, as if reading from some universal rulebook. "It's tradition!"

Emma wanted to argue that it was the 1990s, not the 1950s, but she swallowed her words like she'd been doing since the beginning.

She went back to the bridal shops, this time with Laura. She found a white dress in a style that she genuinely loved, though it wasn't her original dream gown. She wondered what other dreams and goals she would have that Chad would shatter bit by bit.

Even though Emma was wedding-dress shopping, she was still having doubts about marrying Chad. Standing in the bridal salon, surrounded by tulle and satin, she felt a knot in her stomach that wouldn't go away. The consultant gushed about how beautiful she looked, but all she could think about was the fight she and Chad had had the night before. And over something so trivial—the wedding invitation font, of all things. How his face had changed, becoming someone she didn't recognize for a few terrifying seconds.

But she couldn't trust her gut instincts that it was wrong or that it wasn't going well. Every time that voice inside her whispered, "Run," another voice, louder and more insistent, would counter with, "Don't be dramatic" or "Every relationship has problems." She'd invested so much already. Backing out now would mean admitting failure and facing everyone's questions and pity.

Thanks to Chad's interference with her workout routine, she counted calories obsessively, determined to be the perfect size for the big day. The dress would fit perfectly—she'd make sure of it.

Every wedding detail became a battle. The one victory Emma claimed was keeping the wedding in New York. She chose a venue she loved, an elegant space that only hosted one celebration at a time. Despite Chad's vocal disapproval, Emma insisted on silk flowers so they would not wilt. It was a practical decision she refused to back down from, though she paid for it with days of cold silence from him.

Emma wasn't sure which was worse: when Chad insulted her and yelled or when he froze her out. She feared making a decision without him that would backfire later on.

Taking control where she could, Emma paid for her bridesmaids' hair and makeup herself. She'd been to too many weddings where last-minute DIY disasters had added unnecessary stress. She also rebelled against the tradition of identical bridesmaid dresses, having worn her share of expensive satin nightmares that hung in closets until guilt allowed their disposal.

Instead, she allowed her sisters-in-law, whom she adored, to choose their dresses and colors. This decision made Chad clench his jaw, but he couldn't reasonably argue against it since they were from his side of the family.

The morning of the wedding, Emma orchestrated her finest performance. When her bridesmaids gathered to help with the veil, she produced award-worthy tears over the store having forgotten to deliver it. Her friends rushed to comfort her, and she felt a tiny spark of triumph inside. This one small act of defiance made her smile secretly.

Walking down the stairs to the chapel room filled Emma with growing trepidation. Emma's gut instincts told her this marriage was a mistake, but the momentum seemed impossible to stop. She kept thinking once they got married, things would improve. She did not know enough then to trust herself. Too many people had invested time and money, and many expectations hung in the air. She told herself she was just being dramatic, that everything would settle once they were married. Looking back, she would recognize these thoughts as desperate attempts to ignore reality.

CHAPTER SEVEN

THE WEDDING

Though Emma rarely drank alcohol, on her wedding day, she accepted every glass offered by the attentive waitstaff who treated her like royalty. The champagne created a bubble where Chad's disapproving glares and barely contained rage couldn't reach her. She floated in artificial happiness for a few precious hours, surrounded by friends and family who had no idea of the truth behind her bright smile. Each sip dulled the edges of his sharp comments made about her "embarrassing" toast from her college friend, who told about her dress strap slipping during photos and about how much the band was costing per hour.

She navigated the reception like an actress in a play, hitting her marks—first dance, father-daughter dance, cake cutting—while inside, she felt utterly detached from the celebration swirling around her. The liquid courage in her system was the only thing keeping her from breaking character. When her mother commented on her drinking, Emma just laughed it off. "It's my wedding day!" she exclaimed with forced brightness, taking another sip to wash down the lie.

As the night progressed, she found herself seeking refuge in conversations with distant relatives and her husband's business associates—people who required only small talk and polite smiles. Anywhere Chad wasn't. She volunteered to check on elderly guests, to help her flower girl with her sash, and to inspect the dessert table—creating missions that kept her in motion and away from his orbit. When they were forced together for photos, she fixed her smile in place and held her breath, counting the seconds until she could slip away again.

The bubble burst the moment they left the reception. Outside Emma's apartment, gathering luggage for their honeymoon, Chad exploded because she placed a suitcase one inch away from where he thought it should be on the sidewalk.

Their wedding night wasn't romantic or celebratory. It was the beginning of the end, though Emma wouldn't admit that to herself for many months. As she lay in their hotel room that night, listening to Chad's angry breathing beside her, she realized that she had made a huge mistake.

At thirty years old, Emma had been painfully naive about love. She'd grown up on rom-coms where love conquered all, where difficult men were transformed by the right woman's love. No one had ever taught her about emotional abuse or coercive control. Emma's parents divorced when she was two years old. She had no model for a healthy marriage, and she knew that "marriage takes work," but nobody specified what kind of work was normal and what kind was something else entirely.

She had no idea how complicated, expensive, and emotionally draining divorce would be. In her innocence, she'd thought that if things ever got truly unbearable, she could simply walk away. She didn't understand about joint bank accounts that could be emptied, about the legal entanglements of shared property, or about how courts could drag proceedings out for years. She didn't know about the shame that would come with admitting failure so soon, or how skillfully Chad would manipulate his family into believing she was the unstable one.

That night, as Chad's back faced her in cold silence—punishment for dancing "too long" with her cousin at the reception—she still believed that things would improve once they settled into married life. That this was just a rough patch. That marriage counseling could fix anything. Such innocent, misplaced hope from a young woman who had never seen the dark side of love, who still believed that relationships were supposed to be hard, confusing the pain of abuse with the normal growing pains of commitment.

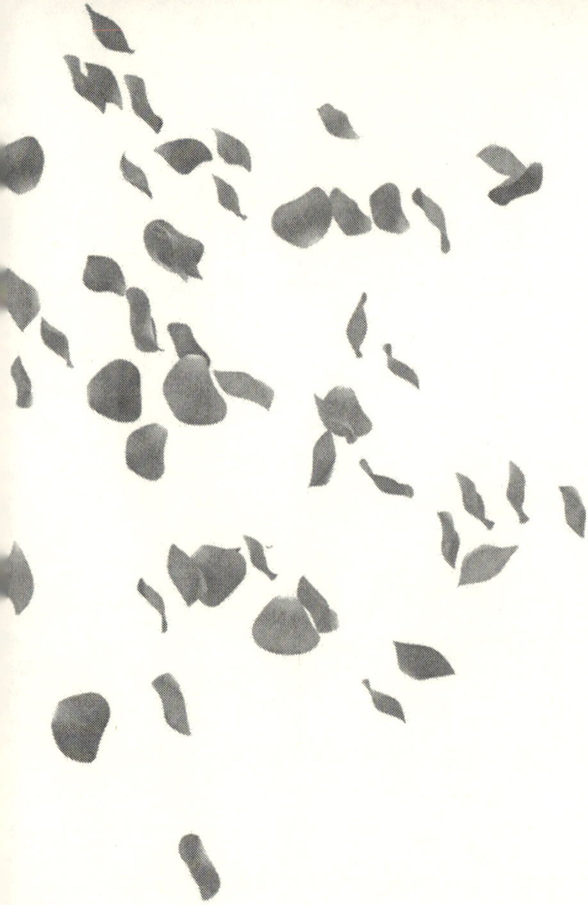

CHAPTER EIGHT

THE HONEYMOON

Emma and Chad went on a honeymoon to Mexico. From the moment they stepped off the plane into the sweltering July heat, Chad's complaints began. He was angry that everybody spoke Spanish. The taxi driver, the hotel receptionist, and the waiters—their natural language was somehow a personal affront to him.

"Why can't they just speak English? We're paying customers," he hissed after checking in, as if the entire country should change to accommodate him.

He did not want Emma, who was a Spanish teacher, to speak Spanish to anyone there. When she thanked their server in perfect Spanish at dinner, Chad's face darkened like an approaching storm. Later, in their suite, he exploded.

"Are you trying to embarrass me? Showing off like that?" he demanded, pacing the tile floor while Emma sat rigid on the edge of the bed.

"It's polite to speak their language," she said quietly.

"It's unnecessary," he snapped back. "And I noticed how that bartender smiled at you."

He was jealous of the staff. The young man who brought fresh towels to their cabana, the tour guide who complimented Emma's pronunciation, and the chef who asked about her interest in local cuisine—all became targets of Chad's suspicion and resentment. His eyes followed her every interaction, his jaw tightening with each friendly exchange.

Chad blamed Emma for the heat. The scorching temperatures, the humidity that hung in the air like a wet blanket—somehow, these, too, became her responsibility.

"You just had to pick Mexico in July, didn't you?" he snarled as sweat beaded on his forehead during their walk on the beach. "Couldn't have chosen somewhere reasonable."

"You selected the destination," Emma reminded him, her voice barely audible above the crashing waves.

"Only because you kept going on about wanting to use your Spanish," he countered, rewriting history as easily as the tide erased footprints in the sand.

Everything was her fault. The sunburn he got after refusing to reapply sunscreen when she suggested it. The food poisoning he claimed to have after eating at a restaurant she'd researched. The rainstorm that interrupted their sunset cruise. His misery became her burden to bear.

He insisted she wear her hair down when it was overwhelmingly hot. Her neck burned and itched, perspiration making her dark curls stick to her skin, but Chad insisted.

"I hate it when you wear it up. You look like a librarian," he said, pulling out her hair tie without asking. "I married a beautiful woman, not someone who looks like she's given up."

For spite, Emma got her hair trimmed and had a spa day with a massage, a manicure, and a pedicure that cost a small fortune. Chad's face when she returned to their room was worth every penny of the $400 charge to their room.

She did everything she could to avoid him. Sunrise yoga on the beach while he slept off his nightly tequilas. A cooking class she signed up for while he nursed his hangover. Shopping trips in the local markets where she could lose herself in crowds and colors and conversations in rapid Spanish that he couldn't understand or control.

They went snorkeling and speedboat riding, but Chad took the joy out of everything. "The water's too salty," he complained during snorkeling. "These fish are nothing special." On the speedboat, it was, "They're going too fast," then "This is boring. Tell them to go faster." His dissatisfaction was a hungry beast that nothing could satisfy.

Emma hated being isolated because of his complaining and insulting toward the people there. She cringed when he spoke loudly and slowly to the housekeeping staff, as if volume could bridge the language gap. She left extra tips in their room, and she gave silent apologies for his behavior. At night, she would stand on their balcony alone, looking at the moon reflected on the Gulf waters, wondering how she was supposed to spend a lifetime with someone who could turn paradise into prison.

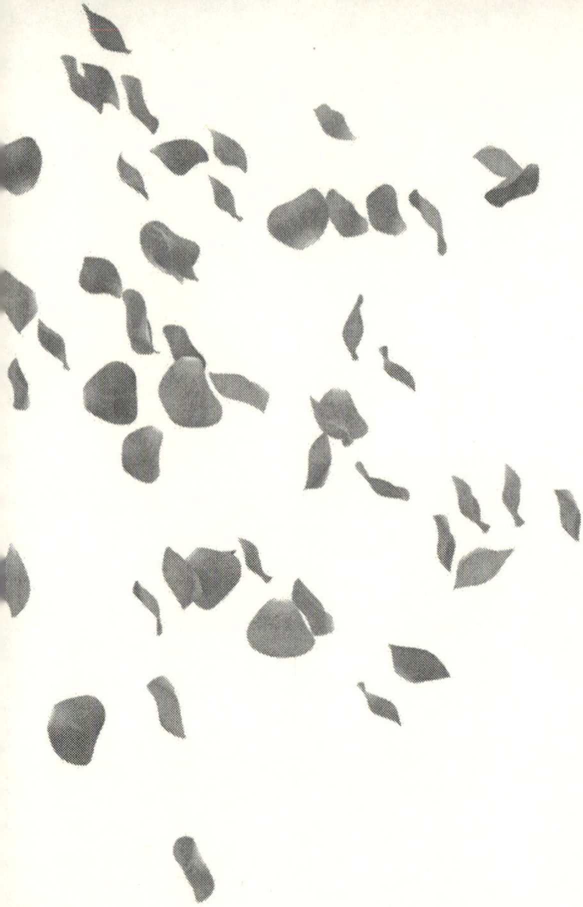

CHAPTER NINE

BACK HOME IN CONNECTICUT

Emma went food shopping on the first day at home after their so-called honeymoon. She loved a particular brand of whole wheat bread, so she bought it. Chad lost it in front of his family, who had just arrived to welcome them home. His face turned red as he berated her for not buying the store brand, which would have cost 50 cents less. The veins in his neck bulged as he lectured her about fiscal responsibility. It was not until later, after their divorce, that she realized the penny-pinching was just about control of her.

Together, Chad and Emma earned enough money to pay their rent. Neither made much, but their small apartment did not cause them financial stress. Despite this fact, Chad had turned every purchase into a battle.

Emma planned a trip home to Queens to see her best friend, Laura. It was like a prison break, and Emma had looked forward to it for weeks. She imagined the freedom. Queens was seventy miles away, and even bumper-to-bumper traffic on I-95 was better than being with him.

Chad's voice carried that familiar, condescending tone on the morning of her trip. He said they needed to discuss their finances and her overspending. Again with the fifty cents for the bread! She hated being spoken to as if she were in kindergarten. Her hands clenched under the table as he droned on, but to make the trip, she had to appease him.

Chad went over every penny in their budget, his red pen scratching across their bank statements like an accusation.

When Emma shopped for new clothing, she hid it in her car, tags still attached, like contraband. She needed new clothes. Having been miserably married and emotionally eating, she had gained weight despite her daily gym routine, another fact that Chad never failed to comment on.

Chad would ask about every pair of shoes and each dress, his eyes narrowing with suspicion. "Is that new?"

And she'd lie, the words bitter on her tongue. "Of course not!"

Each lie added another brick to the wall growing between them. As a teacher, Emma enjoyed shopping for her professional outfits for work. Retail therapy temporarily provided solace—the few moments in a mall without him were peaceful.

After poring over their credit card bills and itemizing each egg and container of milk, it was too late to make the trip to Queens. The traffic would have been insurmountable at the hour that they finished. Emma was heartbroken, sitting in their kitchen with unshed tears burning her eyes. She realized that Chad had done this intentionally to keep her from going, but what could she say?

Arguing with him was a daily occurrence, and Emma did not have the strength. She pretended to go food shopping and called Laura from the car, her voice shaking as she gripped the steering wheel. Her dear friend told her that he was controlling and abusive. Emma had no idea there was a word for her unhappy existence, but hearing it named somehow made it more accurate and survivable.

Chad hated his job as an accountant. Somehow, through twisted logic, it became her fault that he didn't enjoy his career—even though they'd met long after he'd chosen this path. The long hours hunched over spreadsheets left him with a permanent curve to his shoulders and a perpetual scowl. He despised the monotony of tax seasons, the demanding clients who couldn't organize their receipts, and the partners at his firm who passed him over for promotion twice. Every morning, he'd put on his Brooks Brothers suit like armor, his Windsor-knotted tie a noose around his neck, and drag himself to an office he described as "soul-crushing" and "where dreams go to die."

His father, a successful corporate attorney, had pushed him toward accounting—a "practical choice" for someone without the academic drive for law school. The disappointment of settling had festered inside him for years, turning to resentment that poisoned everything it touched. He hated the younger associates with their MBAs from prestigious schools, their ease with the newest software, their ambition that mirrored what he'd once had and somehow lost along the way.

"If I didn't have to support us, I could have tried something else," he'd say, ignoring that Emma's teaching salary contributed significantly to their household. "If you hadn't pushed for this house, this neighborhood, I could take a risk and start over." The blame shifted to her shoulders like everything else, another invisible weight she carried through their marriage.

When the tax season ended each April, Emma hoped for a reprieve from his bitterness. Instead, the temporary relief only highlighted how much he loathed returning to the office in May, making the cycle of resentment begin anew.

Chapter Ten

COOKING AND CLEANING

Since Emma had been a vegan for years before meeting Chad, she only cooked for herself. She ate oatmeal for breakfast and salads for lunch at school, and dinner was simple, too. It was usually a frozen dinner with steamed veggies or tofu from the Chinese place down the block. But Chad? Chad wanted multiple-course meals every night—complete with meat as the centerpiece.

They went out on Friday nights, supposedly giving her a night off. Emma looked forward to not cooking, but the reality was different. Every restaurant choice she made and every word she said was scrutinized under Chad's critical gaze, which made the outings anything but pleasant.

Emma learned to sit across from Chad in silence to avoid the inevitable arguments and tears that followed any attempt at conversation. She stopped sharing stories about her day.

She loved her high school students. Of course, having never taught, Chad had no concept of how emotionally, mentally, and physically exhausting teaching high school was for her. He also constantly belittled her education, telling her she'd gotten her degrees from a cereal box. The irony that she held a master's degree while he held a bachelor's degree didn't seem to occur to him. He could have returned to school for his MBA but didn't, so that was his choice—one he seemed determined to make her pay for.

Chad's latest fixation was avoiding carbs, convinced it was the secret to maintaining his physique. Great. Making a multicourse, low-carb, meat-centered meal every day was a nightmare. Emma taught all day, rushed home to change for her gym class, and she was already completely drained when she returned to cook dinner. Chad would threaten to throw the plate against the wall if he didn't like what she made.

What Emma hated more than the endless cleanup was handling raw meat. The blood, fat, and visible veins made everything seem so viscerally real—because it was! This torment seemed to bring Chad a perverse satisfaction, adding another layer of dread to her daily existence.

Everything Emma believed in or cared about was eroding, piece by piece. Some mornings she barely recognized the woman staring back at her in the mirror. Had she not been so young, her body might have buckled under the constant stress.

Saturdays brought another kind of nightmare. Chad never washed a dish or folded a single piece of laundry. Instead, every Saturday, Emma was expected to transform their apartment into a showroom, scrubbing it from top to bottom.

His family habitually dropped by unannounced, so everything had to be pristine. Though Emma genuinely loved visits from his family, the relentless cleaning was exhausting, and Chad's refusal to help only fueled her growing resentment.

Sundays were reserved for his family. Emma cherished these moments with her in-laws, finding brief respite in their company. Occasionally, she was granted permission to see one of her sisters-in-law alone—what a rare treat, free from Chad's murderous glares and paranoid fears that she might reveal how her life had become a living hell. Emma had long since given up on seeing her own family or friends from back home. Chad always found a way to sabotage those plans, or she paid dearly for them later.

Emma didn't own an iron or ironing board when they first met. Why not? She'd joked it was against her religion. Now, Chad insisted—clearly out of spite—that she iron his clothes. Though Emma lived in the modern world, day by day, bit by bit, Chad was dragging her back to the era of the Stepford Wives. How fitting since she was now living in Connecticut. The only things missing were an apron and pumps while baking bread in their pristine kitchen!

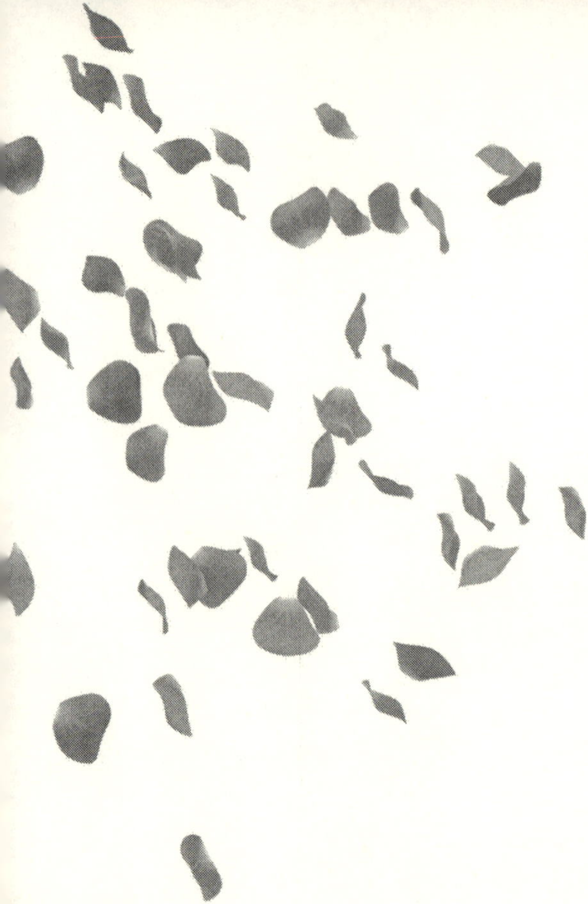

CHAPTER ELEVEN

DAILY LIFE

Emma cherished the two hours she was awake on weekends before he got up. It was a relief not to hear she was stupid, fat, or ugly—immature insults a first grader could have come up with, but they occurred daily and wore her down. Being called a pig for leaving an alleged crumb in the sink after doing the dishes insults the poor animals, Emma thought. They were cleaner and brighter than Chad.

Emma poured over her textbooks in any free moment to prepare for school. She had never taught high school before and had three levels to prepare for. With teenagers, you need to fill every second of your class time well and ensure that they're learning what they need to know. A thirty-year-old should have more fun in her life, but poor Emma's was drudgery.

She would go to the gym and then delay going straight home. Emma swore she would have kept driving past their house if not for her beloved cats. Even a stop for coffee would lead to an interrogation. "Why were you whoring around? Who were you with?!"

Emma was not with anyone. She chose an all-women's gym to appease his jealousy, but nothing worked. She mapped out her escape plan on the back of a receipt while breathing the air of freedom.

Emma hated and dreaded every second she had to be alone with him. She read a lot of books. She discovered their public library and found that, for some inexplicable reason, he left her alone when she was reading. The longer the novel, the better.

Her only brother, Alan, lived out of state in Indiana. He left her alone and had never said anything negative about Chad. The day that Emma left, she called her brother and told him. Alan was a man of few words. His response to the news was telling. He said, "Good."

Chad made any friends' visits so awkward that she decided to avoid her father too. She didn't want her family to see her broken-down state. Chad's hostility was prevalent, and Emma was embarrassed.

Whenever Emma tried to see a friend from work, Chad found a way to keep her home. If she managed to visit Laura or go out with a coworker, the "whoring around" comments lasted for days. Slowly, Emma shut down and isolated herself: work, the gym, and home.

Miraculously, the only people Emma could see without repercussions were Chad's family. She loved her sisters-in-law and brothers-in-law. They were fun to be around, and unlike Chad, they were kind and sweet. She also had nieces and nephews, and they were great to hang out with. Emma spent as much time as possible with her new family.

When Chad accompanied her, the looks of disapproval from across the room let her know there would be, as he said, "Hell to pay later." Emma took that chance. Those few hours were worth it. Or were they?

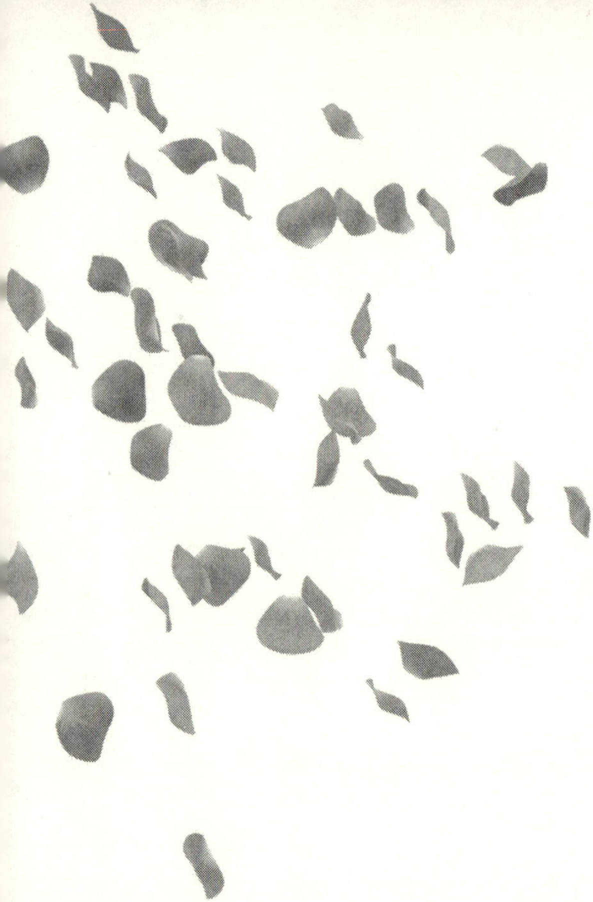

CHAPTER TWELVE

THE ESCAPE

While Chad was out, Emma called her friends John and Kim to ensure they could watch her cats, Oscar and Ziggy. Then she called Laura for help to leave the next day. Laura and Emma made a plan to meet at the diner on I-95.

The day before her departure, Emma had an unplanned wisdom tooth pulled. She had gauze in her mouth to absorb the blood—the metallic taste a constant reminder of her hurry. It was still bleeding on the day. The physical pain was intense, but with each heartbeat, Emma's desire to flee was more significant than any discomfort her body could throw at her.

Chad had pretended to go to an appointment in the morning since he suspected she was up to something. Emma met Laura and her husband, Michael, at their usual diner on I-95. Her jaw was still aching, but her determination was stronger than ever. Emma was not afraid to admit that she feared Chad's temper and that having Michael there would be an asset.

They went apartment hunting using old-school newspaper ads, circling possibilities with shaking hands. Within a couple of hours, Emma found an apartment building she loved near the high school where she worked.

The super said the new apartment wouldn't be ready for two weeks. Emma didn't care since she could stay with Laura in the meantime. It was summer, so school was out for a few more weeks. Emma signed a lease—her signature wobbly but decisive.

Emma, Laura, and Michael returned to the apartment to pack her things; the air thick with tension. Chad returned while they were packing; his heavy footsteps sent Emma's heart racing. He started yelling and accusing Emma of having an affair with Michael—typical paranoid behavior she'd endured for too long. She forced herself to ignore him, focusing instead on the task. Laura and Michael were dragging her giant computer to the car along with her filled black garbage bags full of clothing and books, each representing another step toward freedom.

Lastly, Emma needed to take her petrified cats with her—Oscar and Ziggy, her faithful companions through Chad's volatility. The cat carriers were in the attic, and she needed a ladder from the garage.

Chad wanted to talk instead and reconcile, his voice switching to the false sweetness Emma had grown to distrust. She felt a surge of strength she didn't know she had. Emma told him to get the fucking ladder or Laura would call the police to help her. He obliged, and she coaxed her frightened cats out from under the couch, whispering that they would all be okay.

While Michael and Laura took all her things to their home, Emma drove straight to John and Kim's apartment with her cats, her heart pounding with fear and exhilaration. It was surreal, but she had done it! She was free!

Chad called and emailed innumerable times, but Emma did not respond.

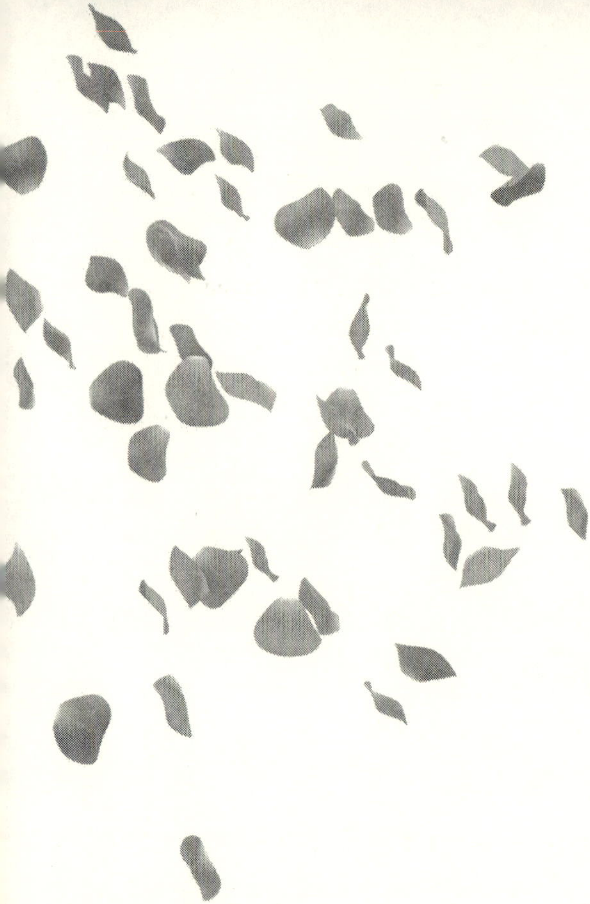

CHAPTER THIRTEEN

AFTER SHE FLED

Once her new apartment was ready, Emma returned to Connecticut since school was about to start again after the summer break. Going back to work gave her a sense of purpose and normalcy she desperately needed. Emma bought some IKEA furniture, which Michael helped her assemble. The fresh lavender scent of new beginnings filled her space.

Emma had left with only her clothing, cats, and the computer. She didn't take any furniture from her old life. It had terrible memories, and she couldn't bear to look at it. Anything that reminded her of Chad was gone, and each new piece she bought represented another small victory in reclaiming her life.

The cats were never his, and she could not remember him petting them even once during their three years together—a fact that spoke volumes about his character. Oscar and Ziggy had always known that their instincts were more perceptive than their mom's judgment.

Although Chad had never actually struck her, the threat lingered in every room they had shared, in every raised voice, in every tensed muscle. She was sure that sooner rather than later, he would have hurt her. In her quieter moments, when she caught her reflection in her new mirrors, she knew with chilling certainty that he would have tried to kill her as she found her voice and courage. Her escape hadn't just been about leaving—it had been about surviving.

She hired a top-notch divorce attorney. Chad was served with the papers but, of course, waited until the last day to file. While Emma impatiently waited for his attorney's reply, Chad kept sending bouquets of roses to her high school. She never read the cards that came with them. He mailed letters with corny cliches to her, too—she sent them back "Return to Sender" unopened.

The flowers became extravagant gifts for her coworkers, who were happy to enjoy them. Roses were her favorite flower, but the thought of them being from him repulsed her. Emma told everybody about Chad's abuse and threats. She made sure to tell the police in the town where she lived and worked, too. Her safety was more important than her privacy and embarrassment.

Once Chad and his attorney responded, he got petty. He asked for only one of the pots and pans they received as a wedding gift to deliberately break up the set. He also wanted his engagement ring back and half of her pension. Then Emma had to go after half his pension, which made his ludicrous request disappear from the proceedings quickly. The ostentatious engagement ring was a marital gift.

"TFB," her lawyer had said.

"Too fucking bad?"

"Yes," he replied.

Emma exclaimed, "I love it!" and knew she had chosen the perfect attorney. Finally, they reached a semi-agreement and went to court.

While waiting outside the courtroom, Emma's attorney told her he was dying to meet this adonis. Emma spit up her coffee! It was the first time she had laughed in months—the sound strange but welcome in her throat.

Emma giggled during the court proceedings as her lawyer said, "And Ms. Emma Davenport will return one pot with cover, Your Honor, to Mr. Davenport!"

Chad's attorney, a woman, tried to shake Emma's hand. Emma told her that representing a monster like him was repugnant, and no, thank you. Finding her voice that day, she told his lawyer that she should be ashamed of herself for representing a client like him.

Next, Emma and her mom traded in her car, which Chad had driven more than his own. Not because he preferred it but because he didn't. Chad saved his gas mileage and beat up her car instead. First, Emma went with Laura to sell the engagement ring Chad had asked for in their divorce settlement. He did not get it because it was a "marital gift."

The ring was worth eighteen of the final nineteen car payments left on her Chevy Cavalier, which she traded in to buy a new RAV4. Her new vehicle, license plates, and the world knowing her secret gave her some sense of safety and peace.

In less than six months, they were divorced. Emma anchored herself to her teaching position, finding solace in the routine and purpose it provided. The day after she left Laura and Michael's, she returned to veganism and had a fridge of her own—small victories that felt enormous.

One of her happiest memories was getting Oscar and Ziggy back! John and Kim kept her cats safe until she could pick them up. Oscar and Ziggy were eleven when she left her marriage, but they both lived to be eighteen years old. Those boys lit up Emma's existence, and she relied on them for love and support, which they gave her unconditionally. Their purrs and gentle headbutts reminded her that she'd made the right choice.

Emma's one-room studio apartment was small and ugly. It did not receive sun because it was in the building's courtyard. Usually, the darkness would have bothered her, but she was not picky after her ordeal. She kept the blinds open so her cats could see outside.

A sunlit one-bedroom apartment became available on a higher floor only a year later. And Emma took it.

Chad's control had involved incessant cleanliness. Emma had done all the household chores alone. Moving to a larger apartment meant more space and responsibilities, but she was ready. Each room she cleaned now was an act of self-care rather than submission, and each decision about where to place furniture was a small celebration of her independence.

PART 2

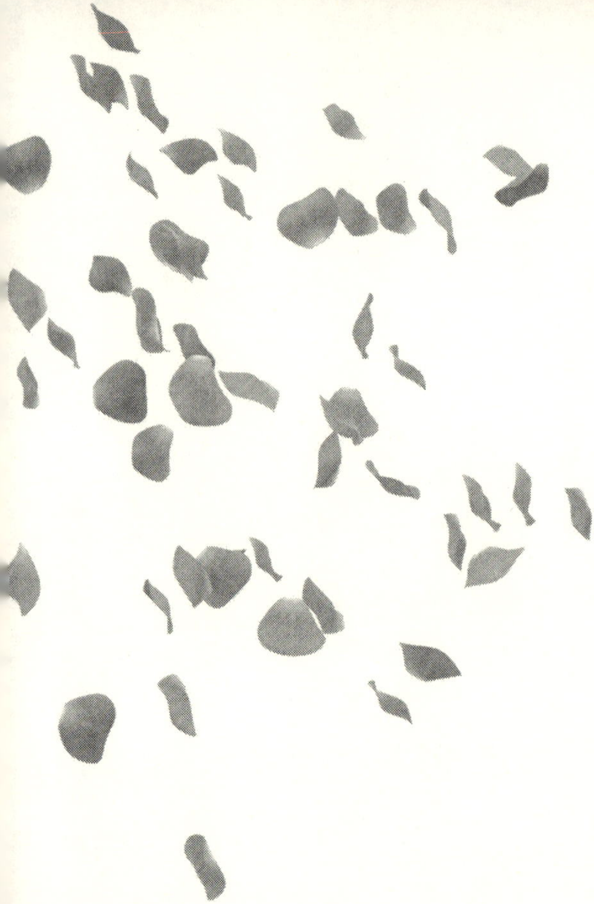

CHAPTER FOURTEEN

HEALING: A JOURNEY OF SELF-DISCOVERY

Emma had found her apartment the same morning that she left Chad. On the second day, she went gym hunting until she found the perfect one. A new class she discovered was boxing. Pounding the bag made her smile.

Emma had been to therapy sessions since she was a teenager, but she didn't go for the three years she was married.

Emma could not see her mom because her mother had stopped speaking to her on her wedding day. They did not talk or see one another until the day Emma left Chad.

Emma had a complicated, dysfunctional relationship with her mother. From childhood, their bond had been built on Emma's constant need for approval and her mother's conditional love. Her mother wielded affection like a weapon, offering it when Emma complied with her wishes and withdrawing it completely when Emma showed any independence.

When Emma announced her engagement to Chad, her mother's disapproval was immediate and absolute. "He'll never be good enough for you," she'd said, though what she meant was, "He'll take you away from me."

The tension escalated until her wedding day, when her mother delivered her final ultimatum. "If you marry him, you're choosing him over me." True to her word, her mother cut all contact after the ceremony, leaving a void that Emma had desperately tried to fill with her marriage.

Losing her mother was difficult in ways Emma couldn't articulate, even to herself. The one year of silence had been a constant gnawing pain. Despite Chad's emotional manipulation and increasing control over her life, part of Emma still craved her mother's validation above all else.

She knew her mother had hated Chad. She had seen it in her eyes long before Emma herself recognized the signs of his possessiveness and isolation tactics. It was difficult to admit, but her mother had been right about him, though perhaps for the wrong reasons. Her mother hadn't been concerned about Emma's well-being as much as about maintaining her control over her daughter's life.

The only way to have her mom back in her life would be to leave him, a realization that filled Emma with both hope and dread. Hope for reconciliation, and dread that she would merely be trading one unhealthy relationship for another. Still, when she finally gathered the courage to pack her bags, her mother was the first person she called, knowing the phone would be answered this time.

But Emma wanted to know why she was in a relationship with Chad when she knew there was no love. She needed to figure out how she wound up with somebody like him. She was an educated and relatively capable person. How did this happen? She also knew that therapy meant finding out. And . . . did she want to know?

One day at the gym, she was speaking to her friend, who had a recommendation for an excellent therapist. When Emma poured her heart out for the first time in his office, she couldn't stop sobbing as she spoke. Emma went once a week to see Dr. Gray. He listened intently and then spurted out pearls of wisdom that made Emma's eyes light up. Instead of feeling helpless, she felt better and stronger each time she left.

Emma found out that her boxing instructor at the gym was a black belt in taekwondo. No wonder she was so impressive in class! Emma grilled her about it but decided that the lessons her gym instructor studied at her dojang were held too far from her apartment to attend.

When Emma told Dr. Gray she was considering taekwondo classes but was petrified, he told her that if she wanted to grow, she would have to come out of her comfort zone.

Emma had seen the J.Lo movie *Enough*, in which her character's husband is physically and emotionally abusive to her. J.Lo goes on the run, and during that time, she hires an expert martial arts instructor to teach her self-defense. J.Lo was Emma's idol; the idea of studying martial arts stuck in her mind.

Emma searched for a martial arts studio closer to home. One Saturday morning, with trepidation, Emma entered the Baekho Taekwondo Dojang. The Korean name means "white tiger"—symbolizing strength, courage, and resilience. There are four gods of direction in Korean traditional culture. A white tiger is the god of the west side of the world. South Korean people believe that white tigers can protect humans from evil, and a white tiger has wisdom, strong muscles, and speed to catch evil ghosts and monsters. Emma loved this name and its meaning.

Emma signed herself up for a special month-long trial. With it, she received a baggy white uniform that was not so attractive. She never wore white except on her wedding day under duress. The uniform is part of the taekwondo culture. She was used to working out in sleeveless tanks, and this heavy long-sleeved material made her uncomfortable, but she sucked it up.

The white cotton uniform felt stiff and awkward against her skin as she fumbled, trying to remember how the instructor had demonstrated tying the belt. The women's changing room was empty, which somehow made it worse—no one to ask for help or share an encouraging smile.

Emma caught a glimpse of herself in the mirror and barely recognized the person staring back—a thirty-year-old woman playing dress-up in pristine white pajamas, her face flushed with embarrassment. The sleeve bore a crisp fold mark from the package, and the pants were slightly too long, pooling around her ankles.

Boxing was fun; the only rule was not to accidentally punch your partner or hit yourself in the face. Taekwondo was more serious. Before each class began, the students had to kneel before the American and South Korean flags and repeat a mantra: "I foster an indomitable spirit."

Emma quickly learned that "cannot" was no longer in her vocabulary.

The taekwondo classes were at night. Emma got up at 6 a.m. for school. After work, she went home, had something to eat, and watched daytime TV while grading her high school students' papers or making new lesson plans. Classes were at 7 p.m., and in the cold and dark of winter, it was difficult to leave her cozy apartment, but she did it three nights a week plus on weekend mornings.

Emma had to learn forms, such as memorizing kicks and punches. If she made a footstep incorrectly, she would have to start from scratch. Her instructors constantly reminded her, "Your other right foot" or "Your other left hand."

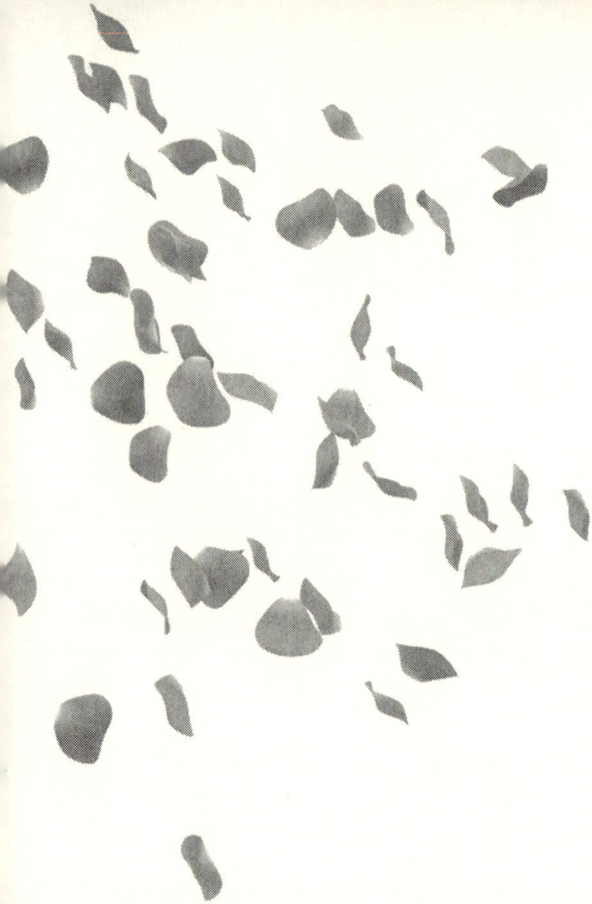

CHAPTER FIFTEEN

BREAKING THROUGH

Emma had to do her white belt form perfectly during her first martial arts test. She practiced so often that it became muscle memory, but she was still nervous.

Emma went alone to her first belt test. At the end, she was asked to punch through a board. What? She thought that was only in the movies. Taekwondo was mind over matter. She forgot that the board was wooden and punched right in the middle. She did it! Emma broke the board in half with her fist! She felt invincible!

Emma took the first board she split in her taekwondo class—a solid pine board that cracked straight down the middle with her perfect punch—and had it framed professionally in a sleek black shadowbox. Then she hung it up proudly at the front door of her apartment, right where everyone could see it!

It was a sign of her growth from timid to empowered and a not-so-subtle warning to any gentleman callers who may come knocking. After what happened with her ex, she decided she would never be afraid again in her own home. Emma smiled with quiet satisfaction every time she looked at that board, running her fingers over the smooth frame and remembering the feeling of breaking through her limitations.

When Emma tried to date years after her divorce, she found that most men she met were emasculated by her martial arts and boxing talents. They wanted her to have longer nails (she needed them short to make a fist in her gloves) and longer hair. Emma knew what that meant. No, thank you! She was better off alone than dating insecure men.

CHAPTER SIXTEEN

UNCOVERING THE TRUTH

Emma continued attending therapy and her taekwondo classes several times a week without fail. Bit by bit, day by day, she grew stronger emotionally and physically. During treatment, she was determined to understand how she had ended up with somebody like Chad—the most demanding challenge she'd ever faced.

Emma had been a selective mute as a young girl. She remembers people asking her mother if she could talk. She had needed a speech pathologist in kindergarten and first grade to learn how to articulate and enunciate. Back then, she only spoke to her mom and brother, Alan. After her divorce, Emma had chosen a male therapist on purpose. All her therapists in New York had been women chosen by her mother. Whenever one of Emma's therapists told her mom that she and Emma were codependent, her mother pulled her out and into another therapy practice. She knew she didn't trust men, but she didn't know why; choosing a man to counsel her was her first step to healing on that front. Emma was determined to tell the truth, find out answers, and learn from them without any interference this time.

The realization was crushing—she had experienced inappropriate touching and boundary violations at four years old by a worker at her preschool who frightened her into silence. The childhood trauma had rendered her voiceless, explaining why she became a selective mute in her early years.

Dr. Gray confirmed the connection between being mute as a young girl and Emma's talkativeness now. She was making up for lost time. It was no accident.

CHAPTER SEVENTEEN

AFTERWARD

Nowadays, things are different. Emma is bilingual. She had studied Spanish in junior high school at the age of twelve. It was a requirement in New York City public schools. Emma loved her Spanish classes. She was required to take a test in New York to graduate from high school, so she continued studying it. And she decided to study Spanish again in college, not because it was a requirement but because she had an inexplicable passion for it.

ONLINE DATING WAS STILL IN ITS INFANCY IN THE EARLY 2000s, but Emma quickly learned to stick to coffee dates after enduring a few awkward dinners with no graceful escape route.

The disasters piled up. Once, Emma received a picture of a handsome young man in his military uniform. When she arrived, she found herself face-to-face with a racist who was bald, heavy, and twenty years older than his photo. She walked out without hesitation.

Then there was the fellow teacher. Though not her type in his profile picture, he'd been kind and funny on the phone. Living just a town apart, they met for coffee. The man who showed up was obese and spent their date ranting about being catfished by a woman who'd used a model's photo when she was actually overweight. Given his deception, the irony of his complaint wasn't lost on Emma. She sat through the date politely but never returned his calls.

The final straw was George, who initially seemed promising because he shared Emma's political views. Breaking her rule of one quick phone call and a few private messages, she allowed him to call her every night for a week before they met in person. She knew better—that mental connections could form only to find out there's zero chemistry when meeting in person. She wasn't shallow, but attraction mattered.

They agreed to meet for coffee at Barnes & Noble on a Friday in the early evening. Emma, with her long strawberry blonde hair and petite five-foot-three frame, matched her current profile photo exactly. George, however, appeared quite different from his picture of a slim, fit man with dark brown hair. In person, his hair was salt and pepper, and he'd filled out considerably. Emma might have overlooked the dated photo, enjoying their easy banter, but before she could even pull out her chair, George declared, "I hope you won't mind my honesty. You're not my type at all."

Emma wanted to scream at him, but the words stuck in her throat. For once in her life, she said nothing. She walked away, waiting until she reached her car to let the tears fall. At least she'd dodged a bullet. What an asshole!

After George's crushing rudeness, Emma was resigned to her mother's "optimistic" prediction that she'd die alone. Life with her cats, the gym, and her job wouldn't be so bad. She had a handful of supportive friends, her mom, and her brother. It was enough. The mortifying experience with George was just the final push she needed to swear off online dating for good.

But Emma had gained something far more valuable than a relationship—she had found herself. Through martial arts, therapy, and self-discovery, she transformed from victim to survivor, from weak to strong, from fearful to fierce. The journey wasn't about finding someone else but about finding herself.

Her friends insisted she was giving up on online dating too quickly. Laura tried setting her up with Michael's coworkers and friends, but Emma wasn't interested in résumés; she wanted someone who "got" her. She saw red flags in every disapproving look or comment, having ignored them all with Chad just because she was turning thirty, and in the 1990s, that had meant marriage.

But this was the 2000s. Now, Emma preferred solitude to poor company. After her marriage, a quiet evening with Oscar and Ziggy became her idea of perfection. Those two furballs lived to be eighteen years old, and their unconditional love was all she needed.

Sadly, first, Ziggy got sick, and three weeks later, Oscar died of a broken heart and kidney failure. They were littermates, thick as thieves. They would playfight and then curl up in one ball together. Oscar was Emma's snuggle bug. He would put his paws on her shoulders, and she could walk around with him everywhere. If he wasn't hugging her, he had to be on her lap or at least have one paw touching her.

Emma found out that Ziggy had cancer and only days to live. He was suffering, so she let him go. She sobbed nonstop for days. Then she realized that Oscar was failing, too. She had always wondered who would be less painful to lose first, but now she knew—neither of them. Letting go of Oscar left her heart shattered in pieces.

Emma was sobbing at work when her friend James, one of the guidance counselors, told her that adopting and rescuing a new kitten or cat was not replacing Ziggy or Oscar. Emma could only sit on the floor and cry in her apartment. She thought she would be happier without the occasional yowling meows in the middle of the night, but it was eerily quiet. And the silence she usually enjoyed was deafening now.

Emma went to the pet store to donate unused cat toys and uneaten food to the rescue team. She could not endure this loss again, so she decided . . . no more cats. However, while she was there, she saw a pair of young black-and-white tuxedo cats.

Emma thought these two were gorgeous. She remembered asking Dr. Gray if she deserved to have such good-looking cats as even that seemed too much. They were rescues, just like her first two fur babies. Fifi was practically climbing out of her enclosure to get Emma's attention.

An employee from the store offered to call Lucy, who arranged the adoption of the cats. Emma said, "No, thank you. I'm just looking."

He called Lucy anyway, and she arrived at the pet store. "Would you like to hold them?" Lucy asked.

Reluctantly, Emma held them. They were three months old and weighed three pounds each. These tiny creatures were adorable.

Typically, Lucy had to run the adoption by the rescue team's president, but seeing that Emma was a cat lover, she told her to return that evening for them. Had Emma said she was adopting them? Emma couldn't remember, but yes, Emma wanted these two babies. When she went back that evening, the rescue team president was there. She saw Emma's tattoo honoring Ziggy and Oscar's lives and knew Lucy had made the right move.

Emma gave it a lot of thought before naming them. Google was not what it is now, but it did exist. As an English major, she loved alliteration and finally decided on Felix and Fifi. Fifi was the first female cat she had. Fifi was a diva. Felix was a mushy and affectionate little bugger. Emma thought Oscar had been the most endearing cat she had ever lived with, but Felix was proving to be lovable and her new cuddle bug. Fifi became Emma's shadow. When they were three-pounders, they both sat on her lap together. This habit continued even when they were fully grown. Chad would have been furious. *Fabulous thought.*

One day on Facebook, Emma thought she saw her old high school crush, Carl. Emma reached out to ask him if he was her friend Carl, and it was! They were now in their forties but talked on the phone for hours. He was still in Queens, and Emma's apartment in Connecticut was a trip, but Carl told her he'd make the I-95 journey.

Emma learned right away that Carl had stage IV cancer. He had been going for treatments and had regular appointments, but she knew the inevitable was coming at some point.

One day, Carl announced that he would go skydiving since he had nothing to lose. Carl asked her to go, too. Even the thought of a roller coaster normally sent Emma's heart racing in all the wrong ways, her palms instantly slick with cold sweat. To support Carl and to overcome her limitations, Emma said, "Yes!"

Emma did not sleep the night before. She had given her apartment keys to a friend from the gym who loved cats. Emma informed her that if she did not call by that evening, she should feed the cats and find them new homes. Perhaps a bit melodramatic!

Emma heard weird noises from her car on the morning of the trip to Queens. For the first time in her life, she had a flat tire. She was on the I-95, and AAA did not come on the highway! Several people stopped to help, but they were all a little creepy. She called Carl, and he came and fixed the flat.

Someone else may have seen the flat tire as an omen and turned around. Nope. Emma was going with Carl to jump out of a plane. Off they went. An hour and a half later, they arrived at the end of Long Island to go skydiving, but there was yet another obstacle.

The wind was off, so they had to miss their scheduled jump time and wait all day until they could take off. Emma didn't want to eat anything for fear of throwing up. Finally, it was time to jump. Emma had imagined there would be some training and instructions. Nope.

Emma was given her parachute and had it put on with her instructor, Peter. They boarded the plane, and Peter connected himself to her harness and parachute. They were going to jump from 13,000 feet up. Most people see thirteen as an unlucky number, but it was one of Emma's favorite numbers. That was a good sign.

Another instructor opened the door and exclaimed, "We are not leaving yet, but we just want some fresh air!" This exclamation lightened the mood.

When Emma and Peter arrived at the open door, Peter told her, "I am going to count to three," and then Peter jumped! There was no warning, which was probably for the best, since she would have tried to back out of it.

Martial arts had nothing on skydiving! Emma was free-falling at about 120 miles per hour for almost a minute, and it was terrifying and exhilarating.

At this point, supporting Carl was her number-one criterion, but anything she did after leaving Chad was a royal "fuck you" to him. Buying brand-name bread, breaking a board, and flying in the clouds were all signs of freedom and growth. The symbolism of her freedom was not lost on Emma.

When they reached the ground, Emma trembled from fear and felt relieved to land in one piece. She smirked, knowing Chad would never have gone skydiving with her. First, it was fun. Second, Chad was afraid of flying. That's why their first wedding anniversary trip was supposed to be a cruise. Nine years after she left, the thought of him made her a little unnerved, but not enough to ruin the moment.

Before Carl died, they parted company. It turned out that Carl had preferred Emma as a young teenager when she was enamored with him and barely spoke for fear of saying the wrong thing. Carl didn't like the adult and healed version of Emma—strong and confident.

Emma was never going to be submissive again. As a child, she'd had no voice, and then again with Chad. When Carl wanted her to stop going to her boxing gym, Emma did not think twice. It was her sanctuary, and there was no way she could stop what she loved for him or any other man. Emma could not continue spending time with Carl, which left her heartbroken.

Emma sat on the phone with Laura from morning until sunset, crying over losing Carl twice. She loved Carl from their teenage years, but this new man was not who she remembered. She was grateful that they had spent time together before he passed away, and it brought closure.

Chapter Eighteen

MOVING ON

Emma decided to fulfill her dream of having indoor garage parking and a more modern apartment than the one she had been living in. With her mom's financial help, she put a three-month deposit on a rental in her dream building. Being a teacher was rewarding but not lucrative—her salary barely kept pace with inflation.

Emma had lived in her first post-divorce apartment building for almost a decade. So, after leaving Chad, the familiar brick facade and creaky elevator had become her security blanket. It felt strange to leave her haven, but watching the younger residents move in and out over the years made her realize it was time for a change.

A week after moving into her new place, an unprecedented storm hit—a bizarre mix of hurricane-force winds and wet, heavy snow that brought down power lines across the state. Emma tried to make the best of it, methodically unpacking boxes in the fading daylight until darkness enveloped her new home.

The temperature dropped rapidly without heat, and the prospect of no hot water for a shower before work tomorrow loomed large. It wasn't ideal, but as Emma huddled under two blankets, she reflected on her years with Chad—the constant criticism and the subtle manipulation. Even this cold, dark apartment felt warmer than those memories.

Emma sat with Felix and Fifi for what she jokingly called their nightly family meeting. It was just the three of them without television or the Internet to distract them. The cats were purring contentedly on her lap, their body heat providing welcome warmth.

Had Emma been at her old building, she would have had neighbors to commiserate with—Mrs. Chen, who always had extra candles, and Peter from 4B, who knew everyone's name and kept track of who needed help during emergencies since he was an EMT. Emma was alone here, surrounded by closed doors and silence.

The isolation felt heavy, but she reminded herself that solitude differed from loneliness. After years of Chad's suffocating presence, she'd learned to appreciate the peace of making decisions without considering anyone else's moods or demands.

Over the next few months, Emma got used to her new building. The real estate agent had marketed it as "luxury," which made Emma laugh now. The building had been considered luxurious when it was built in 1972, but now it showed its age in the slightly worn carpet in the hallways and the dated lobby decor. Still, she loved that two entire walls were windows, floor-to-ceiling glass panels that slid horizontally like patio doors rather than lifting like traditional windows. The view wasn't spectacular—just the street and some trees—but the natural light transformed the space.

She especially loved that the laundry room was on her floor. It might only be one washer and one dryer, shared with three other units, but after a decade of dragging her laundry basket down three flights of stairs to a musty basement laundry room, this felt like a luxury she'd earned. She'd set up a small folding table and started bringing work to grade while waiting for her clothes, making the time productive.

Emma had found contentment in her solitary life. Felix and Fifi kept her company, her students filled her days with purpose, and her apartment, dated as it was, had become the living space she needed. Sometimes, she realized, peace comes not from getting everything you dreamed of but from learning to appreciate what you have.

Emma's fitness journey had evolved over time. She'd started out originally with boxing classes at her regular gym, where her instructor carefully monitored the classes, and it was structured for the average fitness enthusiast like Emma. Later, while seeking to challenge herself, she'd ventured into martial arts—specifically taekwondo—pushing beyond her comfort zone. Emma had to spar with other classmates during her taekwondo classes. Sparring entailed fighting your partner with protective gear and rules to control oneself, but sometimes others did not know their own strength or the desire to win the match overrode the rules of maintaining control at all times.

But now, Emma took up boxing seriously after leaving martial arts. She found an all-boxing gym where heavy bags hung from the ceiling like silent sentinels, their black vinyl surfaces bearing the marks of countless strikes. Making contact with her fists felt liberating—all the power of martial arts without the unpredictability of a sparring partner. Emma was tired of black-belt men side-kicking her into a wall during practice matches, their egos more dangerous than their technique. The late-night classes and accumulating bruises had begun to wear on her both physically and mentally.

Boxing offered something martial arts couldn't: complete control. Punching a heavy bag was straightforward and solitary. It was just Emma and something that couldn't hurt her back. She could swing as hard as she wanted, push herself until her arms ached with satisfying fatigue, but at the end of the day, the bag remained exactly where it was supposed to be. Unlike the unpredictable humans she'd sparred with—who sometimes forgot their strength or let competitive instincts override safety—the heavy bag was predictable, consistent, and, ultimately, safe. Here, she could build strength and confidence without fear of being thrown or struck unexpectedly.

By this point, Emma had been in martial arts classes for eight years, learning the intricate dance of combat. As she got older, the late-night classes started affecting her entire existence—waking up exhausted from teaching and drinking too much coffee to stay alert.

Emma left the White Tiger as a brown belt, just one level beneath the black belt, with newfound self-confidence that radiated from her movements. The techniques were ingrained in her muscle memory: how to block a punch, grab an attacker, and strike with her free hand. While Emma hoped she would never need these skills, her photographic memory stored each technique like entries in a deadly encyclopedia. Most importantly, she no longer lived in a constant state of hypervigilance.

Her days fell into a comfortable rhythm. She would teach all day, her mind already anticipating the evening workout. As soon as the final bell rang, she would fly home, feed her cats Felix and Fifi, and rush to her boxing gym, barely having time to change. The classes ran from 4:45 to 5:45, the perfect time to release the day's tensions.

Everything changed when another boxing gym in the franchise closed without warning. The owner disappeared one night, leaving confused and angry members who began infiltrating Emma's space. She bristled at the disruption to her carefully established routine.

Then she noticed him among the transferees—a man with a handsome face and blue eyes that crinkled when he smiled. He looked kind, but Emma's initial instinct was to dismiss him as another rich snob like Chad; this was, after all, an affluent area.

She had deliberately chosen a gym far from her high school, having learned the hard way about maintaining boundaries between her work life and her private one. Emma had run into her high school students, past and present, at her previous gyms who wanted to chitchat. She wanted to leave her job at the high school and not bring it to the gym, which was meant to help her decompress after a long day.

With this man, the conversations between classes were brief but promising. There were fifteen minutes between her class ending and his beginning, giving them only precious minutes to chat while they switched places at the punching bags. Emma's past experiences with deceptive men—those who conveniently forgot their wedding rings during workouts or lied about live-in girlfriends—had left her skeptical. Will didn't seem like a liar, but she had lost faith in her ability to judge character.

One day, he extended his hand. "Hi, I'm Will," he said, his palm warm and calloused from hitting the bags. Emma thought the formal introduction seemed more than casually friendly, but she refused to get her hopes up.

The next time she saw him, he wore a Mets shirt—the blue and orange as familiar to her as her reflection. Growing up five minutes from the stadium had made Emma a lifelong fan, and she seized the chance to connect.

"You're a Mets fan?" she asked rhetorically, then added, "We're probably the only two fans around here." Feeling like a babbling teenager, she quickly said, "Good night," and fled, her face burning with embarrassment.

Their pleasant exchanges continued for a month before Christmas Eve. As a teacher, Emma had the day off for the holiday. She had only seen Will during weekday evenings and Saturday mornings, when they both looked considerably more alert. Christmas fell on a Tuesday that year, with a special ninety-minute class. Will's unexpected presence was a welcome surprise.

Tired of uncertainty gnawing at her, Emma asked one of their instructors, Evan, to discreetly find out if he was taken. Emma figured he was, and she just wanted to rip off the Band-Aid. She assumed Evan, being in his forties like Emma, would handle it with maturity—unlike the high school kids Emma taught. That assumption proved wildly incorrect.

Evan approached the situation with all the subtlety of a soap opera character. He cornered Will's friend, Jonathan, and asked point-blank if Will had a girlfriend or wife. "He's single," Jonathan revealed, "and he has a huge crush on that member named Emma."

Evan's expression transformed with matchmaking glee. He wasted no time. While Will was focused on his workout, punching the bag with a steady rhythm, Evan strode over. "She likes you too," he announced. "Ask her out, and she'll say yes. Merry Christmas!" Then he walked away, leaving Will shy and confused, his rhythm on the bag completely thrown off.

Emma remained oblivious to this exchange. After class, Jonathan lingered nearby, preventing any private conversation. All Emma and Will could manage was a rushed "Merry Christmas!" before walking away, the holiday air thick with unspoken words.

As a teacher, Emma had a week off from school during the holidays. Instead of waiting until her evening boxing sessions, she went in the mornings. Without exchanging numbers, Will and Emma lost a week to talk or hang out. They finally saw each other again that weekend during their shared morning class.

Thankfully, Will was shy and not a player. "Do you want to do something later?" he asked hesitantly.

"Yes." She asked Will for his phone to put in her number, but he hesitated without explanation. Emma assumed it was in his truck. She got a piece of scrap paper from the front desk and wrote it down.

That afternoon, an unexpected snowstorm blanketed the area. Will didn't call to confirm their date until later in the day. Emma was already cozy on her couch with Felix and Fifi, absorbed in a Hallmark holiday movie. She would rather not venture out in the snow. When Will called, she asked if they could postpone until the following day because of the weather. His simple "Okay" and abrupt hang-up left her wondering.

However, he called her the next day, and they made plans to go to a local restaurant. Emma had assumed he lived near the gym, but surprisingly, he lived just three miles down the same road from her. He was refreshingly down-to-earth—nothing like Chad's stuffiness.

Emma loved living in her luxury building with Jeff, the doorman, who knew her by name. When Will arrived, Jeff asked him to wait in the lobby while Emma received the customary phone call announcing her guest's arrival. She could get used to this.

On previous dates—though she hadn't been on one with someone new in years—Emma had worried obsessively about her appearance, words, everything. Chad had only intensified her self-consciousness. But having resigned herself to a life alone with Felix and Fifi, she decided to be herself. It had worked with Will at the boxing sessions so far, so why not continue?

Emma had cut her hair into a short bob years ago. Without Chad measuring the length of her hair, she felt it suited her better. The shorter length was also practical for her daily gym workouts and teaching schedule. Will had only seen her in workout clothes, sweating through boxing classes—never dressed, with makeup and her hair done.

Will opened the truck door for her—something Chad had never done. Over dinner, their conversation flowed easily and naturally. When she ordered a beer, Emma remembered countless dates where men had lectured her about beer not being feminine, insisting she should drink wine instead. She hated wine!

Will wore casual jeans and a regular shirt—not a polo. Emma had discussed in therapy how she needed someone who didn't remind her of Chad, and Will was checking all the boxes!

But Emma had something to confess to Will—she was vegan. After her prior experiences, she braced herself for this to be the end of their journey. It wasn't.

Instead, Will shared stories about rescuing a baby squirrel he'd named Rocky and nursing him back to health before bringing him to a sanctuary. He told her about adopting his late uncle's dog, rescuing his cat Dusty from inside a car's hood, and caring for his fish, snake, and bird. Emma felt her heart warm, knowing he truly loved animals, too.

The contrast with Chad was stark. When Chad had discovered Emma was a vegan, he'd gone ballistic, belittling her and threatening to end things if she didn't "fit in" by eating meat again. Will asked her about her veganism with genuine interest.

Emma explained how she'd become a vegan out of love for animals and not wanting to harm them.

In therapy, Dr. Gray helped her understand that following her principles would also help her sleep better at night.

With Whole Foods just ten minutes from her apartment and Trader Joe's a few miles further, Emma committed fully to veganism. Back then, vegan options were scarce. While cooking at home was easy, eating out meant carefully modified salads—hold the chicken, cheese, and bacon bits. Will listened without judgment or criticism. How refreshing!

Then Will made his confession—he didn't own a cell phone. Emma was stunned—everyone had one these days. He explained that his family had offered to add him to their plan, but he'd refused. The idea of being constantly accessible made him uncomfortable.

Instead of feeling foolish, Emma felt relief. They both had quirks, but these differences brought them closer rather than drove them apart. Will's gentleness and kindness helped Emma relax into a new, unfamiliar feeling of ease. Though her past experiences made her wary of optimism, she tried to stay positive.

Will waited a couple of days to call again, later admitting he hadn't wanted to seem too eager. When he did call, he asked her out for the following weekend—and specifically mentioned getting himself a cell phone.

He chose a restaurant with vegan options, a thoughtful gesture that overwhelmed Emma—no one had ever shown such consideration before.

First, they went to the Verizon store, where Will picked out the latest iPhone, wanting the best. Their dinner afterward at Park & Orchard was smooth and relaxed, like their first date. The restaurant was fancy and elegant, serving a delicious vegan lasagna made entirely from vegetables. Will maintained his gentlemanly manner right through dropping her off at her building.

The next day, while Emma attended a cycling class at her other gym and Will went to the boxing gym, she broke the rules. She texted Will, thanking him for their date and asking about his plans. He was free, so they met for lunch at a local diner and saw a movie afterward.

Sitting in the theater, Emma realized she hadn't been to a movie with a man since Chad a decade ago. But this was different. Will's hand was warm in hers, and the usual tension was absent. Even watching a movie with Chad had been an ordeal—if he didn't like the plot, somehow it had been her fault. Now, in the darkened theater with Will, Emma felt something she hadn't experienced in years—peace.

Will called Emma every night for weeks, a new routine that shifted their usually early bedtimes into hours of conversation that stretched late into the evening. Emma, determined not to repeat past mistakes, laid all her cards on the table. Instead of waiting for Will to discover her complexities over time, she chose to be direct about her past trauma and the people she had needed to cut from her life. Will's response surprised her—he listened with genuine concern, offered sympathy without judgment, and, most importantly, didn't retreat.

She revealed more of herself: her love for children despite her decision not to have any of her own, a choice influenced by her selective mutism stemming from childhood trauma. Teaching had become her way of nurturing and helping children daily. At forty-something, she felt at peace with this decision. Will's response was again refreshingly honest—he, too, didn't want children. When Emma insisted she wasn't just saying this to please him with plans to change her mind later, he understood and respected her sincerity.

Their relationship deepened naturally. When one of Emma's respected colleagues announced their retirement, she invited Will to the celebration party, fully expecting him to decline. Instead, his response touched her heart: "I will do anything to spend more time with you." The evening revealed an unexpected connection—the teachers Will was about to meet had once been his own.

Though Emma arrived at the high school two decades after his graduation, preventing impropriety, it created an amusing web of connections. Will and his siblings had impeccable reputations, adding to Emma's comfort.

These connections would later prove valuable when they renovated their home together. Emma found reliable contractors through her students' and colleagues' husbands and fathers—people who had grown up in their tight-knit community. Their shared history made the entire process smoother.

The next milestone came naturally: meeting the parents. Will arrived at Emma's mother's house bearing flowers—a gesture that, while touching, wasn't what won her over. Emma's mom was a painter, and she painted those flowers, so it was clear that she loved them. It was Will's genuine kindness and sincere love for Emma that earned her mother's unprecedented approval.

Emma met Will's family at his aunt's eightieth birthday celebration—a full immersion into a gathering of seventy-five close family members, including his mother, stepfather, siblings, nieces, nephews, and cousins. His family's warmth and acceptance helped Emma feel immediately at home.

Unlike her previous relationship with Chad, where every conversation felt like navigating a minefield, discussing marriage with Will felt natural and easy. Within six months, they were engaged, and two months later, they married. Emma's desire for a simple courthouse ceremony—which had caused endless drama with Chad—aligned perfectly with Will's dislike of being the center of attention.

Their Connecticut courthouse wedding was perfect for them. They chose August, deliberately avoiding July—the month of Emma's first wedding that now felt jinxed. As an educator, Emma was always reluctant to take time off during the school year unless necessary, so the timing worked perfectly.

Their small town's judge performed marriages only during his Wednesday lunch hour, creating an intimate ceremony attended by their mothers, who had never met before. The unexpected connection between Will's mom from Brooklyn and Emma's from neighboring Queens, just three years apart in age, filled the day with nostalgic "Do you remember in those days..." conversations.

Emma's wedding dress choice spoke volumes about her growth—a beige, lacy floral 1920s flapper dress that cost just $49 on sale. She smiled, knowing the flappers represented independent women who defied social norms at that time. Emma imagined how Chad would have reacted to its color, style, and length. Will complemented her perfectly in khaki chinos and a baby-blue polo shirt—quintessentially Connecticut casual.

They celebrated afterward with lunch at Park & Orchard, where they'd had their second date. The day was unusually mild for August, overcast but dry. Unlike her first wedding, Emma didn't need alcohol to finish the day. The twenty-eight-dollar marriage license fee became a joke between them—the best money they'd ever spent on starting their life together.

Emma and Will's story wasn't about grand gestures or perfect timing. It was about two people who found each other when they were ready, chose honesty over pretense, and built their relationship on mutual understanding and respect. In Will, Emma found someone who wouldn't try to change her or judge her past. In Emma, Will found someone who appreciated his sincerity and shared his values. Together, they created their definition of a mature and realistic love story.

EPILOGUE

Leaving Chad was one of the most complicated challenges Emma had ever faced, but it wasn't the last mountain she'd climb. The courage to step out of her comfort zone and study martial arts pushed her emotionally and physically, building a strength she never knew she possessed. Though the divorce had been expensive and time-consuming, Emma celebrated her freedom with a lightness in her heart she hadn't felt in years.

Every August 21st, the anniversary of her departure, Emma made a pilgrimage to Pandora and added another charm to her bracelet. By the time Will entered her life a decade later, that bracelet had become a glittering testament to her growth and resilience, each charm telling its own story of healing.

Chad had parked inside their garage while Emma parked out on the street. Chad flew out of their garage in a clean and warm car when there was ice or frost on her windshield or snow to dig out. Emma had to do it herself. With Will, when the world was blanketed in snow, Emma sipped her coffee while he cleaned off and warmed up her car—salting to ensure her safety. What a difference a couple of decades can make.

Valentine's Day with Will meant exchanging cards. They didn't need or want gifts because their love had matured. They may get a couple's massage or have a nice lunch. They weren't pretentious, so getting dressed up was reserved for weddings and funerals. Will always sent flowers to Emma's workplace, but they were to make her smile, not to draw attention to how wonderful he was.

Loving Will showed Emma what a healthy relationship truly meant. When emotions overwhelmed her, Will's steady presence and understanding helped ground her. Unlike Chad, who'd dismissed her feelings and branded her "crazy" for having normal emotional reactions, Will stood firmly by her side, validating her experiences and protecting her right to feel.

They found joy in sharing activities while respecting each other's independence. Boxing became their shared passion, though they learned to balance joint workouts with solo exercise routines over their twelve years together. They could speak to whoever they chose at the gym without repercussions. How refreshing for Emma!

They cherished the TV shows and movies they watched together, but they also found comfort in quiet evenings, sitting side by side on the couch, each lost in their own entertainment with separate headphones.

Their mutual love for animals manifested in a home filled with ten rescued cats, each given free rein over furniture and sleeping spaces. Emma had vivid memories of her cats crying outside Chad's locked bedroom door, and she'd vowed never again to let a man dictate her pets' place in her life.

Their shared passion for animals extended beyond their home. Regular visits to an animal sanctuary became their tradition, where they'd spend hours among cows, pigs, turkeys, chickens, ducks, donkeys, and their favorites—the goats. Emma would smile as they trudged through the farm in their mud-caked boots, knowing Chad would never set foot in such a place.

Will's family had become Emma's sanctuary after losing her parents and brother within just a few years of each other. Where once there had been an emptiness that threatened to swallow her whole, Will's parents, siblings, and their children filled that void with genuine affection and inclusion. They never tried to replace what she had lost but instead created space for her grief while simultaneously weaving her into the fabric of their family traditions. Holiday gatherings at Will's sister's home became anchors in her year, and his mother's daily phone calls offered companionship that required no explanation or apology. Though the ache of losing her biological family never fully disappeared, Emma found profound comfort in knowing she belonged somewhere again, with people who loved her without condition or expectation. And she loved them, too.

Through therapy, Emma had learned that true love wasn't about the butterflies or emotional roller coasters she'd once mistaken for passion. The phrase "You complete me" now struck her as the opposite of healthy love. Genuine relationships, she discovered with Dr. Gray, required two "whole" people coming together as equals, comfortable with both togetherness and separation. No one person could—or should—complete another.

Though Emma had initially sworn off marriage after Chad, she eventually realized that with Will, a marriage license represented something different—mutual respect and partnership. Their relationship wasn't perfect—perfection, she'd learned, was just another word for control and stress. Instead, they had good days and bad, but Emma felt supported and truly loved for who she was through it all.

Their life together was beautifully ordinary, far from the carefully curated drama of social media relationships. Their home echoed only with the demanding meows of attention-seeking cats, and their days flowed in a natural rhythm of togetherness and independence. Unlike the dread accompanying Chad's return home each evening, Emma looked forward to Will's presence at day's end.

Every night, without fail, Will's drowsy "I love you" would float through the darkness. And every night, Emma's heart would fill with gratitude as she responded, "I love you, too."

ACKNOWLEDGMENTS

I WANT TO EXPRESS MY DEEPEST GRATITUDE TO MY HUSBAND, Al, and my dear friend, Laura, for their unwavering love and support. Your encouragement has meant the world to me.

Thank you to R.G., EdD, for helping me reclaim my life. Your guidance and impact will never be forgotten.

Lastly, thank you to Ita, Richard, Dan, Rusty, Robin, Brady and my friends from https://twelveweekbook.com, without whom this book would not be possible.

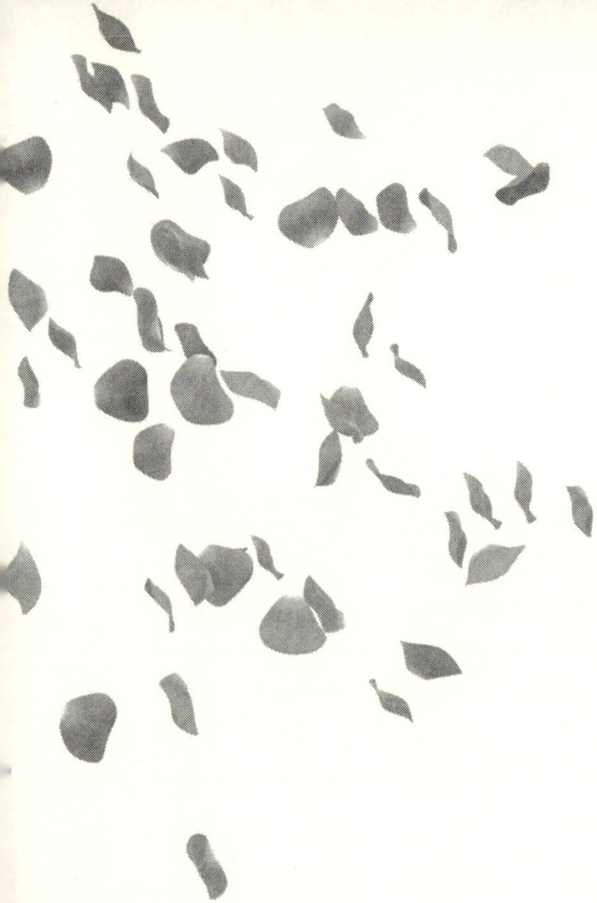

ABOUT THE AUTHOR

Cherie Hans draws from her experiences as a lifelong educator and language enthusiast to infuse authenticity into her storytelling. After decades of teaching Spanish and bilingual education, she now dedicates her time to helping adult learners master English as a second language. Her intimate understanding of language barriers—both literal and metaphorical—shapes her unique perspective on human resilience and transformation.

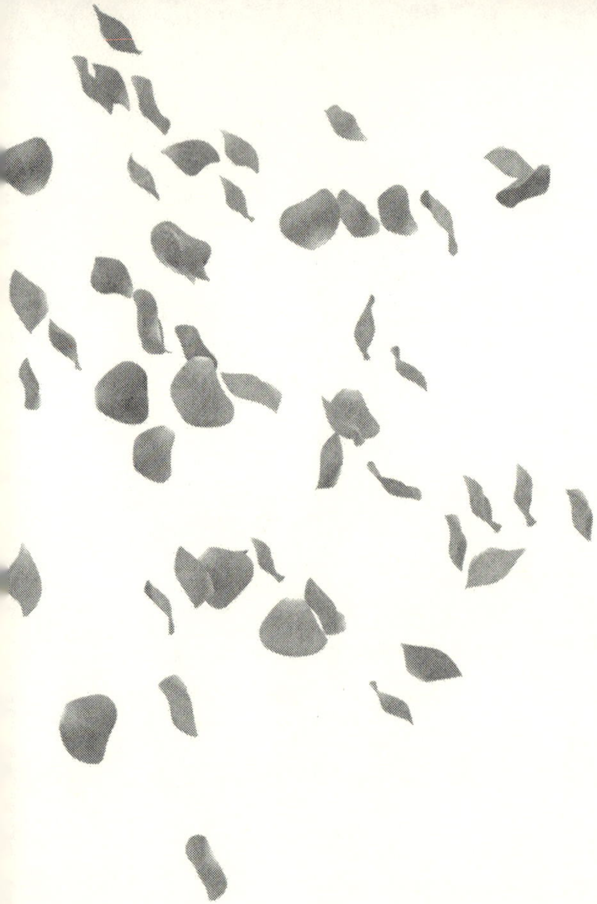

Made in the USA
Columbia, SC
08 April 2025